978-1-105-52707-4
Imprint: Lulu.com

This book is dedicated to my
Language Arts teacher, Mr. Lang.
The epitome of fabulousness,
he is the most amazing teacher
I have ever had.

May 3rd, 2019

Chapter 1

In my world a whip shows the highest social status. For you folks it might be money, or popularity, or even fancy clothing. I think a whip makes more sense because the slave never whips the master, the master whips the slave. Whoever holds the whip is on top. They're the lion, the wolf, the bear. As much as I fear the whip, I don't fear the man holding it. Without it he holds no power over us. Without it, is he even a master?

The tip raked against his back, tearing his musty shirt, shredding his skin, and exposing his crimson blood. Master Banks, the man holding the whip, stared at his slave with a crazed expression. He might have been mistaken for a mad scientist testing some concoction on a rat. I winced every time Master snapped the whip, almost as if I was the one in the chair.

He does this to protect us, I told myself. *It has to be done.*

I've never been outside the plantation, but Master Banks told us it's like living in a wasteland. He said that the world was much better when slavery was legal, back when we didn't have to hide in India. Another slave told me that Master traveled all the way from another continent in a giant flying machine that looked like a bird! Maybe one day I would fly in one of these bird-like contraptions. I hope not, because then I'd have to leave my home and venture into the *w a s t e l a n d.*

Another slave stepped up to the chair and I thought about the first time I had been whipped. If my memory is working,

I was about 3 or 4 years old. Oh man, did I cry. But now I realize this is necessary, as Master Banks tells us, for keeping us slaves in line. One time I heard Master Mah Ahuja telling Master Banks that he thought whipping was awful. Master Banks told him that "it is what it is." I'm not quite sure what that means, but Master Banks told us to stay away from Master Mah after that day.

I guess I should stop rambling and introduce myself. My name is Camille Banks. Before you ask, because I know you will, Master Banks is not my Papa, but he acts like it sometimes. He teaches us how to harvest corn and what-not. Instead of giving us money, he gives us scraps of bread and stalls to sleep in. One slave asked why he don't get no money and Master told him that he is rescuing us from the rest of the world, so we should pay him. He is kind, though, so he don't make us do that.

One day, I want to have a family. Master Banks says that ain't allowed. This one slave wanted to marry this other slave real bad so she asked Master if she could leave the plantation to do so. I guess that slave left, because I never saw her again.

There are about 10 slaves on the plantation, all around 16 years old, like me. Most of us were taken here as babies. From a young age we was told that we wasn't as good as white folks. It took me a while to understand, but I've accepted it.

From what Master told us, our plantation is small compared to most. There's one house, and it's real fancy looking, at least compared to where I sleep. Like I mentioned, all the slaves live in stalls, right next to Master Banks' and Master Mah Ahuja's house. We stay *silent* at night so as not to disturb our Masters. Master Banks told us we will get whipped for 5 times longer if we make noise! I'm okay with that rule. It means I can relax after a day's work and listen to the chirping of the Jerusalem crickets and the gentle sways of the corn in the field.

Regaining my focus on my surroundings, I glanced around the room. There was that chair, where you have to sit backwards on it like you're hugging it so Master could whip you on the back. The walls were illuminated with torches. The flames curled and snapped, as if in sync with the whip, now a mere few feet from me.

The whip was a smaller one, about half the size of me. It began with a short handle, wrapped in black leather. I didn't get to see the tail all that much. If the whip wasn't slashing the air it was locked away in Master Banks' house, but in the few glimpses I caught, it looked dangerous. The tail consisted of a thin black rope with some pieces of wire at the tip. Now that don't seem like it would do more than sting, but it sure does hurt coming at you that fast. There's this one slave, Jeffery, he has these nasty scars up his spine from all the times he tried to run. Long strips of bumpy, reddish skin running up and down the planes of his back. He don't like to take his shirt off much. It seems like a *goonga* idea, running away from the only safe place for us Africans, but I guess he just wanted to be a part of the *wasteland* he calls the outside world.

Only one slave in front of me now. She straddled that chair like her life depended on it, clutching the wooden rails on the back. With a blood-curdling scream, the sharp tail of the whip scraped her skin like a dagger.

After what seemed like a lifetime, the woman stood, tears flowing down her cheeks like a river. I took 7 steps forward, as always. *One, two, three, four, five, six, seven.* Sitting down hard I wrapped my arms around the back like it was my mama. My feet curled around the bottom, the pain of the splintery wood miniscule compared to the whip that would soon be snapped at me. I squeezed my eyes shut and braced myself, more mentally than physically, for what I was about to experience.

Chapter 2

I couldn't see anything but I heard the snap of the whip and felt the honed edge slashing into my skin. It seemed like a million needles were dancing across my back, plucking, pinching, and poking. I felt it rake across me again, once, twice...

"Wait!" I heard a boy shout, uncertainty laced in his tone. The needles quit dancing, at least for a moment. My eyes were still squeezed shut and I didn't dare open them in my state of confusion. Ringing filled my ears like a marching band had inhabited them. Was I imagining this? I kept my eyes and ears closed, blocking out the world, ignoring that anything, *anything,* was happening. I *hated* the confusion.

"What's that, boy?" Said Master Banks, the one who was whipping me, in a not-so-patient tone.

"Banks, he's just a boy. He doesn't know what he's saying!" I recognized that voice. That was Master Mah, the other Master! I heard he had a son… was his son the one that stopped Master Banks from snapping the whip ?

My eyes fluttered open, tired of ignoring the unknown. I turned my head to see a very troubled Master Mah Ahuja, a furious yet composed Master Banks, and a boy, around my age, who I believe was the one who started all this. The boy was tall, with bright red hair that stuck straight up. His skin was lighter than mine, but darker than Master Banks'. He stared straight at Master Mah with warm, dark green eyes that reminded me of corn leaves. His expression was dull, as if his heart was smashed with Shango's hammer. Then I remembered: *he's just a boy. He doesn't know what he's doing!* Those words must hurt coming from his papa.

The boy glanced over at me. For a split second, our eyes met. Even from across the room it felt like we had connected. No, not connected. *Interlocked.*

"What was that, boy?" Master Banks repeated, drawing the boy's attention away from me.

"She... Um... You're hurting her." The boy stood like a superhero with a flowing cape and a mighty sword, except he had none of those things. Those eyes made up for the lack of cape and sword.

"Oh, I'm hurting her? I'm hurting the poor, little girl? Well, son, I DON'T CARE. I don't care that I'm hurting her because I don't care about *her*." Master said *her* as if it were some contagious disease. He said *her* like he meant *it*.

The words didn't sink in. They just

floated on the surface like an empty ship, no meaning, no significance. What did he mean, *he doesn't care about me?*

My thoughts were interrupted when the boy spoke up, "I mean no disrespect sir, but this is wrong!" I felt the passion in his voice. He looked older, more mature, after he said that, despite the fact that his voice jumped up an octave when he said 'wrong'.

"Shut that pathetic little mouth of yours or I'll whip you as well!" Master Banks raged. He was fuming; I could almost see the steam blowing out of his ears. Everyone gawked at the two of them, a sort of lava-like tension bubbling below us. Master Mah, on the other hand, looked like he was going to puke. His expression was miserable, but not surprised. It read more like *regret.*

A wild expression arose upon the boy's face and the whole room seemed to draw in a sharp breath.

Oh no, I thought, despite the fact nothing had happened yet.

With no further consideration, not on what he was doing or why he was doing it, he reached behind him and grabbed a torch. With a thunderous grunt he chucked the ball of flame across the room, sending it flying in Master Banks' direction.

The torch soared through the air but, as it turns out, the boy ain't a good tosser because the torch wasn't headed for Master no more, it was coming straight for me. My eyes widening, I pushed myself (and the chair) to the floor, letting the torch fall to the dry wood. A flaming hot, blistering fire erupted in the room and the flames seemed to grow bigger with every second I watched them. I lay there, horrified, on top of the pieces of the broken chair I once compared to my mama.

To say that the fire was HOT is a complete understatement. I felt sparks pop and fall upon my skin, bringing back the dancing needles. My eyes were watering so badly I could feel tears flow down my cheeks. The fire was a growing force and I needed to get away, but I couldn't. I was stuck, paralyzed, like some garden statue Master Banks puts out in the summer.

It was like the world had fallen still. We all stared at the once miniscule flame, which now covered about the size of a bed, slowly climbing up the wall.

The boy shattered my daze when he grabbed my arm and hauled to my feet. His grip on my arm was firm, but still gentle.

I felt like a pile of pudding and my legs seemed to be in as much shock as the rest of me. Every time I stood up, they collapsed under me.

"Come on!" Archie cried desperately. People were starting to react, but it was too late. The flames had engulfed a good portion of the wood, and smoke had wrapped around my lungs like a rope. From the looks of it the others were feeling the rope tighten, too.

At last I locked my knees, stabilizing myself. We ran out of the building, the boy still clutching my arm. I was about to collapse, and he knew. Stopping momentarily, he scooped me up in his arms and continued to run. I was too exhausted and too desperate to protest. After what seemed like hours he fell to his knees, dropping me onto the sandy, grimy ground. It was as dark as a cave but I could tell we were in some sort of desert. The boy looked like he was going to faint, yet I still bombarded him with questions:

"Who are you? Where are we? Where's the plantation? How do we get home?"

"Jeez, slow down, you're making my head spin!" I scrutinized his head. It wasn't spinning or even slowly turning. I disregarded it.

"Well? You brought me here! The least you can do is answer my questions."

"Relax, Sunshine, I saved your life."

"Oh, you mean you saved me from that fire that you'd gone and started?"

"Whatever. My name's Archie Ahuja, but you can call me Arch," he winked at me.

I rolled my eyes and responded, "My name's Camille. You're Master Mah Ahuja's son, aren't you?"

A look of pure anguish overtook his features. He screeched out, "My father!"

"What about him?"

"I... we were running and I forgot, and I... I left him at the plantation!"

Chapter 3

Tears pooled in his eyes.

"Hey…" I had no idea what to say, so I didn't. I just sat there. The silence was comforting. It was as silent as it was in my stall back home. We stayed sitting like that for a while, the whistle of the wind our only distraction from the darkness of the night.

"Why did you throw that torch?" I finally asked, after a good few minutes of building up the courage.

"Because whipping people is wrong," he pursed his lips, "That's what my dad always told me."

We decided to get some rest. We could

figure out a plan once we weren't so darn exhausted.

As I lay awake, the horror of the situation sunk in. I had left my fellow slaves and disobeyed Master! Oh, I'm sure he'll be real mad!

What if we never go back? What if Archie turns on me and leaves me here? What if the fire… no, no, no! Tears swelled in my eyes, eventually cascading down my cheeks, a miniature waterfall on my face.

My sobs were drowned out by Archie's booming snores. I missed my home. I missed my stall. I missed shucking corn and, heck, I even missed being whipped. Master was right, I ain't ready for the outside world. I tried to stifle my cries as much as possible, because I don't want Archie to see me like this.

In an effort to sleep I drifted back to the past. Even my worst memories seemed safer than this desert.

When I was about 13 I had this friend. Her name was... Abebe, I think? Curses, my remberey ain't working. Anyways, Abebe and I did just about everything together. We shared our bread, did our work together, and we even slept in the same stall. I always found the stall more comfortable when she was there. Abebe was around 17 then. She was a bold gal and always stood up for the other slaves. Master Banks didn't like her too much because she was always trying to teach the other slaves to read. You see, she was taken to the plantation when she was around 7 so she was real smart. One day she taught me how to read the word *free.* Master went crazy on her! He whipped her bloody and screamed that she is just a slave and nothing more. She came to the stall in tears that night and we both fell asleep scared. The next morning she was gone. The stall was empty, except for me, and no signs of her remained. I asked

Master Banks where she went but he just told me that she "had to go." I haven't seen her since, and boy, do I miss her.

~

I guess I cried myself to sleep because the next thing I knew, Archie was shaking my arm and hollering for me to wake! I sat up feeling groggy, quickly wiping my face of dried salt from last night.

"Morning, Sunshine," Archie stood over me, reaching out his hand to help me up. I took it, cautiously. He hauled me up real fast and soon enough I was standing so close to his face that our noses were almost touching! I could feel a bead of sweat rise on my palm, but it was too early in the morning to be hot.

"Thanks," I breathed.

"Yeah, no problem," Archie smiled, stepping away. His cheeks looked as red as Master Banks did when he got mad.

Was Archie mad at me?

"So what's the plan?" I changed the subject.

"Here's the thing, Sunshine," I rolled my eyes at that. "We're in a place called Rajasthan. Right now we're about 50 kilometers from Pakistan. If we cross the border, they won't come after us because slavery is illegeal and it's too risky." Pakistan? He wants me to leave the plantation? No way! He can't just steal me from my home and order me around!

"Wait! No, I can't leave! This is my home, I ain't going!" My breathing grew faster and it felt like my heart was beating out of my chest!

"Slow down, Sunshine! There's another option." Starting to calm down, I kept listening, "We *could* head back. I could save my father, you could stay there, but you must know that Master Banks might kill us." Archie's expression hardened into a grim frown.

"He is kind, Archie. He won't do that to us."

"Yes, he will. But it's up to you. I lose either way."

"What do you mean?"

"If I go back, Banks will beat the crap out of me. If I cross the border, Banks will beat the crap out of my father."

"Oh... Master Banks might go easy on you, being as you're Master Mah's son."

"Yeah. Maybe." We were silent for a moment.

"Archie?"

"Yes, Sunshine?"

"I think I want to go home."

"Ok," Archie murmured, "But I wouldn't call it home anymore." The look on Archie's face was enough to concern me, let alone him telling me that Master is a vengeful monster who will beat us. No, Master isn't like that. I tucked away that thought in the back of my mind, never to be seen again.

Chapter 4

We headed back, Archie leading the way. I had been walking for a while and my feet knew it. They were sore and achy. Archie told me the term for that was *'My dogs are barking.'* I thought that was absurd. I have no dogs, and they are certainly not barking. When I asked him what it meant he shrugged and told me it was just an expression. That confused me even more.

"So Master Mah Ahuha is your father?" I asked, just making some conversation. Archie chuckled, seemingly for no reason.

"What?" I exclaimed.

"It's just, um, it's pronounced

ah-who-ja-" he tried to stifle his laughter, "-not a-hu-ha!" He burst out hysterically laughing. Rolling my eyes, I marched ahead. I was anxious to get back.

"What I was going to say, before you so rudely interrupted me, is why don't you look like your papa?"

He was quiet for a moment. "My dad is from India, which is where we are right now. My mum is from Ireland. Her name is Heather Ciara Ahu*ja*." He smiled at the mention of his mother. "She was wonderful, but she got really sick and we didn't have enough money to pay the medical bills. Banks offered to help with our bills in exchange for running the plantation, and…" he paused, a sorrowful look contorting his face. It was the same expression his father had... *regret*. "My mum was ashamed. She left one night and said she couldn't love my dad anymore." He nodded slowly, as if someone was telling the story to him.

"Oh," I squeaked, not quite sure how to respond. "Archie, your dad's decisions ain't yours. I'm sure your mama still loves you, because you're her son. No matter how hard you try, you can't give up on family. My friend, Abebe, taught me that."

"Thanks, Sunshine. What about you? We've lived on the same farm for years but we've never talked once!"

"You're right, but there ain't much to talk about. I've lived here my whole life."

"So this is the first time you've been outside the plantation?"

"Since I can remember."

Ever since I was little I've always wanted a family of my own. Now I realize that nothing is worth leaving the plantation. This past day has been horrible and I just hope everything will go back to normal. The plantation is my *family.*

As we approached home all my hopes of going back to normal were crushed. The farm was in ruins. Scraps of wood stood half burnt yet still stuck in the ground. A thick layer of ash and soot had settled over just about everything. The cornfield was barely visible and the Masters' house stood unstably, ready to collapse at any second. The sky was grey and dull and all life seemed to have vanished. No one was there. Not a slave, not a master, not even a stalk of corn.

The ash was so dense I could barely see my hands in front of me. I could no longer hear Archie, so I assumed he had wandered off.

I suddenly felt a sharp pain on my bare foot. Crouching, I picked up a dusty rope with a wire end. It was Master's whip!

I started searching through the ash and dust for signs of what had happened. I coughed and coughed, the sound echoing through the desolate land. The wind started to pick up, blowing ash in my eyes and mouth until I couldn't stand it no more. I stood, yelling Archie's name. I kept yelling for a few minutes, to no avail.

My heart sank like a ship in the ocean. I felt more alone than ever. Tears formed in my eyes from dust and panic, making it even more impossible to see.

Then I heard footsteps behind me.

"Archie?" I whispered uneasily, but no one responded. *It's just my imagination,* I tried to convince myself. *I'm home now. I'm safe here.*

Suddenly, I felt hands reach out from behind and heave me off the ground. I screamed and turned my head to see the most terrifying sight I had ever seen.

Master Banks was the one who grabbed me, but it wasn't really him. One side of his face was normal, besides the crazed expression. But the other side… the other side would haunt my worst nightmares. It looked like it had melted right off. His right nostril had been burnt shut. His cheek looked like an overused candle, dripping down his face. He didn't have a right ear no more. In its place was a stump of skin that didn't look like it could do much hearing. His eye was bloodshot and watery, almost as if he had just been crying.

I screamed again, kicking as hard as I could, "Master, please!" My screams broke into sobs as an idea popped into my mind. I reached behind me and hit Banks as hard as I could on the burnt side of his face.

He dropped me instantly, screeching out in pain as his hands reached up to his wounded skin.

"Agh!" The booming scream rang out in the silent air. I ran as fast as my tired feet allowed me, kicking buckets of ash up. My throat hurt real bad. It felt like I had swallowed lava, knives, and wasps, all at the same time.

I tripped over Archie, flying head first into the rubble. His grey shirt blended perfectly with the dull surroundings. I regained my balance, coughing once more.

Looking back, I saw Archie crouching over something… or more like someone.

He was crying real hard. I went to comfort him but when I stepped closer I recognized the man he was crying over: it was Master Mah Ahuja. Master lay on a bed of ash, his eyes closed, no air coming from his lungs. He didn't seem to have any burn marks, unlike Master Banks.

"No, dad!" Archie croaked, his voice as broken as the plantation. "Please!" His sobs must have been heard for miles.

"I need you." He murmured the sentence, like a wounded animal in the woods. I couldn't look him in the eye.

Master Mah whispered, and his heartbroken son put his ear to his papa's mouth. Master spoke again, saying something I couldn't hear. Or maybe I just didn't want to hear? After a moment of silence, Archie nodded, stood, and looked at me, grief-stricken. I didn't think anything I could possibly say would be sufficient, so I reached out and held his ash-covered hand.

We walked away, hand in hand, away from the only home I've ever known.

I walked with a grieving Archie until the sun was rising. I still hadn't said a word. What was I supposed to say? No words could help this situation. I didn't question him on what his father said or tell him about Master Banks, because if my papa died, I'd want to be silent for a long time. And, if I'm being honest, I wasn't wanting to talk much anyways.

Being left alone with my thoughts wasn't ideal, either. While Archie was busy mourning the loss of his father, I was mourning the loss of my home. Archie told me not to call it home, but I had no better option. If the plantation ain't my home, then I got no home at all.

Maybe I should tell Archie about Master Banks. But what's he going to say? *I told you so?* Besides, I wasn't in terms with the fact that the man who I once called my father had attacked me.

I'm being unfair. He was just protecting me, right? Protecting me from the *wasteland?*

But, what if he was attacking me? I mean, I deserve it. He is my Master and I deserve a whipping. I wish Archie never started that fire. Then I would be back in my *home* and everything would be back to *normal.* I wouldn't be out here in the middle of nowhere, leaving my wreck of a home and walking into a place I've been warned not to go my whole life. Resentment built up inside of me, hotter than the flames that destroyed my home. I stopped walking and glared at Archie. He didn't notice my withering stares; he just kept walking, step after step after step. For some reason this irritated me even more.

Chapter 5

"Why did you start that fire?" I demanded.

"It was always burning since the world's been turning," murmured a very solemn Archie, "Harry Truman, Dorris Day, Red China, Jonny Ray." What was he talking about?

As if reading my thoughts, he said, "It's a song. My mum loved it."

"You don't get it, Archie. I had a good life! You don't know, 'cause you've been part of the outside world, but I liked my life! Now you've gone and ruined it all! Now us slaves might have gotten a whipping once in a while, but we was fine! We was more than fine, Archie!"

"We were."

"What now?"

"You said 'we was.' It's 'we were.' Did no one ever teach you proper grammar?"

"No, but-"

"Exactly. You see, *normal* kids go to school and learn these things. But Banks wants to keep you dumb, so he *'don't teach ya nothin'!"*

His words hit me like a falling tree hitting the ground. 'Timber!' my heart yelled. But a small voice somewhere inside told me that it hurt because it's the truth. Something told me that I wasn't mad at Archie. I was mad at something else.

"I'm real sorry," I spat, before I changed my mind. "That anger ain't meant for you."

"Yeah, me too. I think you're really smart, and funny, and nice, and..." he cleared his throat and made his voice lower, "...and, um, I'm sorry."

My face felt like it was burning.

"We need a plan. And a good one." He stated, averting his eyes from mine.

"I'm afraid we don't got many options. We cross the border, or…" I shuddered at the thought of going back to the plantation.

"Okay, so it's settled. We'll cross the border to Pakistan." Archie said it like it was as easy as shucking corn.

"What then?" I questioned. Archie offered no answer.

"We don't got a then, but we do got a now. How far from the border are we?" I answered my own question.

"Not too far. 30 kilometers, maybe?"

"How many days of walking is that?"

"In our state, one or two. Just one problem, I have no clue which way is Pakistan."

"What direction is it?"

"Um… West?"

"Well then, we're headed that way," I

pointed at the now setting sun.

"How'd you know that?"

"I'm not as dumb as you think, *Sunshine,*" I joked, smirking at him. I'm still not sure why Archie calls me Sunshine. I used to roll my eyes at it, but now I just smile.

We headed off, a long journey ahead of us. We was joking and laughing, almost as if we was family. The golden light of the evening fell upon his face, making it look like his skin was glowing.

I'll admit it, Archie looked pretty handsome. His smile was the sun, lighting up the whole field. It was brilliant, and it made my heart expand like a balloon. But we was just friends. *Just friends.*

I didn't know it at the time, but as we enjoyed the evening, a darkness loomed behind us. There was an evil lurking like a panther, ready to pounce at the next opportunity.

Chapter 6

We had been walking for what seemed like ages. The sun had fallen and risen again and still we trudged forward.

We was walking through this hilly area, lush with kelly green grass and thick, full trees when Archie said the luscious landscape reminded him of Ireland. He told me all about the island, from the stone castles to the rocky coasts. Maybe I'll visit Ireland one day. Every fantasy now seems so realistic.

Only about a dozen kilometers to go. We was so close!

"What're you going to do once we're out of India?" Archie asked. That was a tough question. I've never had to think about that before yesterday!

"I dunno. Maybe find another plantation, find someone who can take care of me. I heard there was a lot of them in Pakistan." I thought my answer was reasonable but Archie looked at me as if I was a madman.

"Are you insane? You can't go back to another plantation! That's ridi- You can't just- Ugh!" His brain seemed to be making sentences faster than his mouth could handle.

"What do you want me to do, Archie? How am I supposed to take care of myself?"

"I don't know! Get a job or something!"

"*A job.* That's perfect, Archie. I'll just walk into a shop and ask for a job with no training, no schooling, and no home. I don't got no where else to go!"

"Yeah, well, I don't have a home either but you don't see me running to become a slave!"

"Whatever. Let's just find some water."

"Fine."

We hiked on for a few minutes. Finally, I heard the faint trickle of a stream and I knew we was close to water.

After slurping down handfuls of the precious liquid Archie whined, "I'm starving! Is there any food around here?" He walked over to a berry tree behind us.

"No!" I startled him with my shout. "Those are poisonous. Here, eat these instead." I grabbed some dogwood berries, carefully avoiding the tree because it causes a nasty rash.

"Nice." Archie glanced down at the spiky red berries I held in my palm. He scooped them up, his fingertips brushing my hand gently. Butterflies flapped their wings in my stomach.

"Let's just get to the border, okay? We shouldn't be dilly dallying like this."

"Why? We're only like…" he munched

on some more berries, "a few kilometers away."

"Fine, I guess we can stay for a while longer." The truth is, I ain't doing too good either. My whipping wounds stung, my feet ached, and even after the berries I snacked on, I was *starving.*

I should be saving these berries for later, I told myself. My stomach grumbled in protest.

I've made it this far, I can finish this.

The sun beat down on us, making me even more hot and tired. I had come all this way; I had to cross the border.

"We should really get going."

"Fine!" Archie complained, "Just let me grab some berries for the road."

"Just don't touch the tree!"

We headed off, a few kilometers away from the border. A few kilometers away from a new life.

Chapter 7

I felt a hard push on my back, shoving me to the ground. It hurt like crazy: I was shoved right in the whipping wounds. I fell hard, my mouth suddenly filled with dirt and blood.

"Camille!" Archie cried my name fearfully, but I was too dazed to stand.

"Archie," rasped a familiar voice, "I see you have found the runaway slave." It was Master Banks! My heart beat like a drum. Was this good? Will Master save me? Or will he beat me?

I tried to stand, only for my arms to buckle and fall back into the dirt.

"How did you find us?" Archie asked.

Was he buying me time to run?

I tried once again to stand. This time I crouched, sitting like a frog. I placed my palms down on the ground and slowly lifted myself up.

I turned around to face Master Banks.

"Archie," He said again, ignoring my existence. "Your father is at the plantation awaiting your arrival…"

"My father is dead!" Archie rasped.

"No, no, young Master, he is alive, thanks to me, and waiting for you to bring home a slave." Master Banks glanced over at me like I was some fine meat ready to be eaten.

To my surprise, Archie asked, "He is?"

"Yes, he is, and all you have to do is come back *home*." No, Archie, no! I was in too much shock to say anything.

"Just step... over... here." Archie obeyed Master Banks' command like a well-trained dog.

The devastation hit me. This one boy

who had ruined my whole world and stolen me from my home had now turned against me. I knew it! I knew I never should have trusted him. I never should have left the plantation! I wish everything could go back to the way it used to-

"Camille!" Master's voice interrupted my distressed thoughts.

"Why don't you come back home?" No, no, no! How was I supposed to resist the sweet offer he was about to make?

"I could take you back, you'd get your old stall, and everything could go back to *normal.* I wouldn't want you to end up like Abebe..." It felt like a swarm of hornets built a nest inside my heart. My brain told me to say yes and go back home. This is what I wanted! I had been hoping for this all along!

But another small, annoying part of my heart told me to run, and never stop running until I crossed the border. But I ain't fast enough. They would catch me, and…

No. I couldn't go back there. I had to run.

"Well?" Master Banks was getting impatient.

How dare Archie? He was the one telling me that the plantation ain't my home and I shouldn't go back there. But what do you know, the first chance he gets he's going back. So I am alone, with no family once again.

"Master… I…" I bolted. My feet hit the dirt, *thump, thump, thump, thump,* like my heartbeat. I filled my lungs with the afternoon breeze. I heard the distant shouts of Master Banks demanding that I return. I'd like to say that I never looked back, but I did. *Once.* Master and Archie were both running towards me. Was abandoning me not enough? Was Archie out to get me now?

I kept running.

"Camille, wait!" Archie breathed. Who

was he to tell me to submit myself to him at his command? As I was about to run through a muddy swamp he grabbed my arm and threw me to the side. The action caused him to fall into the mud himself, making a loud *plop* noise. I lay on the ground, barely conscious. My head was throbbing and I felt a warm liquid running down my left arm.

Master Banks approached, but he kept his distance. Why wasn't he grabbing me? He looked me dead in the eye and told me coldly,

"You two aren't worth the trouble. I won't risk my life on a slave. Ha! At this rate, you'll die out here alone. You should have listened, girl, when I told you that you couldn't handle it out here. You're better off on a plantation where you can tell yourself you're loved. Now you have no one!"

"No," Archie croaked from the mud pile.

"What do you mean, *no?*"

"I mean, she does have someone who loves her." He stared straight into my eyes. All my hatred and disappointment towards him vanished with those seven words.

"Oh please, this is coming from a boy whose parents don't even love him."

"Where is my father?"

"Oh, Archie, no. You gullible fool. Your father isn't alive! He's been dead since you left! And you know why he's dead? Because YOU started a fire that killed him. So good luck getting out of that mud pit." Master Banks kicked a rock at Archie, only to have it sink below the mud.

Oh no… Archie's father is- agh! The pain from both of our hearts surrounded us like a deep fog. Too dense to escape, but thin enough that I could catch glimpses of the outside. We was laying there, practically lifeless, weighed down to the ground by Master Banks' words. The bees in my heart seemed to die, leaving me hollow and miserable. What was the point in trying to stand up? Master was right, I can't handle myself. I wish I had taken his offer. Then everything would go back to *normal.*

Chapter 8

Normal? What about my life has been *normal?* Archie told me that normal kids sleep on a bed, and eat more than scraps, and aren't forced to work for 16 straight hours, and aren't told they're worthless. I shouldn't have to live in a world where I am limited by slavery. Banks was wrong, I could handle myself! And Banks... he never cared about me. He stole me from my real family and forced me to live here. He whips me, constantly. Someone who loved me wouldn't do that. Someone who loved me would put a stop to that. Someone like Archie!

I looked over to see my closest friend

sinking into the mud. Quicksand! This is why Banks didn't go after me, he didn't want to get trapped in the sand! My brain was going a mile a minute. I had to save him, but how? I grabbed the closest stick I could find and shoved it towards him.

"Here, take it!" Archie was up to his knees now, yet he made no attempt to grab the stick. His expression was blank and dull, like his mind was in a coma.

"Come on, Archie!" I exclaimed.

"What's the point?" He finally whispered. The mud was up to his waist now, reaching for the rest of his torso.

"Please, you're the closest thing to family I got." I admitted. "I need you." I whispered the words to him softly. Seconds passed. He had no response.

"Please!"

Finally, he grabbed the stick. I pulled, using all the strength I could muster. Archie rose out of the foul pit, inch by inch. Minutes passed. I would pull him out a few inches, then the quicksand would draw him back in. It was a never ending battle.

Nevertheless, I kept pulling. The sand was down to his knees, his jeans caked with the tan liquid.

With a grunt I ripped him out of the quicksand. As we tumbled to the ground, relief washed over me. He was free! And even more… I was free! Not only of slavery but of my dark fears about the outside world. It wasn't a wasteland! In fact, the only opposition I've faced has been from the plantation! I was ready to cross the border.

Chapter 9

After walking in silence for about an hour, Archie spoke up,

“Hey, Camille, I’m sorry for leaving you, and-”

“It’s okay. I forgive you,” I can’t say I got no anger towards him deep within me, but watching him try to apologize made me sad. Besides, he saved me from that quicksand. If he hadn’t pushed me away and fallen in himself, I might be dead. And what use did I have hating on the closest thing to family I got?

“So, when Banks was talking and you was saying *someone* loved me…” My voice trailed off.

"Oh, yeah, haha, that was just, um-"

"Yeah," I smiled, "That's what I thought."

"Anyways, you ready to cross the border?"

"Um-hum," I faltered, "As ready as I'll ever be?" It sounded more like a question than a confident response.

"Hey, what's that?" I pointed at a small, dark line stretching across the horizon, like a slithering snake.

"Where?"

"Look at that line. What is it?"

"Dunno. Guess we'll find out."

We approached a small town that looked real poor, but not poor enough not to give us weird looks. They were warranted, though. Two teenagers, one covered in dried sand, the other barefoot with a bloody arm. Speaking of, my arm was hurting real bad. Archie offered to find some medicine but I refused. We had more important matters at hand.

We walked some more and the snake we were approaching was coming into view. It was a fence, and a big one at that. It was black with barbed wire at the top and people dressed in green uniforms marching around.

"Military." Archie mumbled, "Of course there's military."

"What do we do?

"That's up to you to figure out while I go find some stuff for your arm." He pulled a few dollars out of his jeans pocket.

"Archie, wait-" but he was already gone.

Okay. No big deal. I just need to figure out how to face an entire army. I was doomed.

Archie returned before I had even begun to make a plan.

"I got it!" He exclaimed, waving around some ointment. "Okay, so you distract the guards while I climb over the fence, then I'll take out all the guards and pull you over."

"That ain't *never* going to work."

"Okay, I'll distract them while you climb over and-"

"Or, we could just tell them our situation."

"But then the police will find us and put us in an orphanage and we'll get separated!"

"Then let's tell them, they'll let us through, then we'll cause a distraction and bolt."

"So no taking out the guards?"

"No taking out the guards, Archie."

"Alright, Sunshine, let's do this!"

As we approached, a few guards turned towards us. My heart was booming so loud that I'm surprised they didn't hear it!

"Excuse me, Master-" Archie elbowed me, "Erm, I mean sir, my friend and I are escaping from this plantation and it was real bad and they can't come after us if we're in Pakistan... So, can we get through?"

"ےل ساپ ےک سیلوپ وک ںونود پآ مہ اج ےہر ںیہ," he responded in a low tone. My brow furrowed. Noticing this, another guard stepped forward and said,

"He said that we're taking you two down to the police." Okay, as expected, we were being taken (away from the border, I may say) to a nearby police station in India. But on the bright side, two guards had followed us, so that's two less guards at the border.

We marched, 10 steps, 50 steps, 100 steps, long enough to make them think we was staying.

That's when I shouted, "NOW!" We dashed away. *Run, run, run! Don't stop for anything!* Those five minutes were a sweaty blur. I heard shouts and screams all around us. We was approaching the fence and I felt good. The wind in my hair, the clapering of Archie's footsteps behind me. I ain't stopping for no one!

The guards yelled some more, "Come on, men! Don't let them escape!" This was it. Our plan had failed; they were going to catch us.

Without saying a word, one guard stood. Glancing around at everyone, she held out her right hand and pointed at the ground in front of the guards. She began to circle her hand back and forth. All the guards came to a hesitant halt, waiting for more commands. This may have just been my imagination, but I could have sworn the woman commanding the army winked at me. I saluted quickly before focusing on the task at hand.

I grabbed one of the pickets before she changed her mind. I think it was 10, maybe 11 inches apart? I reached my foot out and stepped down. One foot across the border. Standing sideways, I squeezed in between and, with a push, I stepped through. *I was across the border.* I felt older, and wiser. I felt like I might really have a future. From here, *I* was the one who chose my path.

Archie, on the other hand, didn't have such a graceful entry into the new world.

He tripped over the bottom of the fence, falling face first into the dirt. I hauled him up and we was running once again.

"We made it!" Archie told me cheerfully.

"We ain't out of danger yet. Keep running!"

We ran until we couldn't see the border no more. I was out of breath, and from the looks of it, Archie was even worse…

"Here," he wheezed, "you're arm stuff." He handed over a small bottle of white cream, panting like a dog on a hot day.

"Right. Thanks, by the way." I rubbed the ointment on my arm. It almost instantly eased the pain.

"So," Archie perked up, "we made it!"

Chapter 10

I smiled from ear to ear.

"I'm free! I'm freeee!" I skipped around the dirt covered area we was in.

"What're you going to do now?" Archie asked.

"What are *we* going to do now?" I corrected him.

"Well, why don't we start by getting some rest?" The sun was setting, creating a soft glow around us. We fell asleep with the fine, cool dirt as our bed.

"Archie?" I whispered.

"Yes, Sunshine?"

"I keep thinking about how we're free, but all these other slaves are still stuck, forced to work with no future or nothing!"

Archie was quiet for a moment, then responded, "I know. But don't think about that right now. Think about how you're free and we'll deal with the rest later." He rolled over to sleep.

That night I dreamt of Banks, out there, torturing more slaves. Most dreams you can wake up from. I don't think this will go away when I open my eyes.

The next morning we made a plan: we would head to Balochistan. Archie could teach me how to read and write, we would get jobs and we'd have freedom and a future. My dream was coming true! Archie and I are our own little family.

The nightmare I dreamt of last night still bugs me. I don't think I'll ever be truly happy until Banks is behind bars. I tucked the thought into the back of my mind.

"To Balochistan?" Archie asked, holding out a hand.

"To Balochistan!" I replied as I took his hand.

And so we walked, hand in hand, the sun at our backs, the world at our feet.

Acknowledgements

First of all, thank *you* for making it to the end of the book. Without you I'd have no reason to write this!

Another thank you to all my beta readers: Avery, Garrett, Kathryn, and Abby. They had the thankless job of reading my book and giving me feedback. *Crossing The Line* wouldn't have been nearly as enjoyable to read if it weren't for them.

Thanks to my sister, who I sat and wrote next to as she did her grad school homework. Congrats on graduating!

Thanks to my mom, A.K.A. my Alpha reader.

A huge thank you to my dad, who

doubles as my amazing editor and cover designer. You wouldn't believe the amount of commas he deleted…

Shout out to Abbie Emmons, whose website and videos are abundant with incredibly useful information.

And lastly, I want to thank all my past Language Arts teachers, especially Ms. VanOstrand, who is a magnificent teacher!

Keep an eye out for the next book in the
Crossing The Line trilogy!